J Merrill Publishing, Inc.
434 Hillpine Drive
Columbus, OH 43207
www.JMerrill.pub

Library of Congress Control Number: 2023903839
ISBN-13: 978-1-954414-78-5 (Paperback)
ISBN-13: 978-1-954414-79-2 (eBook)

Book Title: Your brain has too much what, mommy??
Author: Essence Unique
Illustration: Freddie Crocheron

To my miracle baby, my Ezzy. You are the reason for everything. You're my sun and moon. I love you past the stars.

This book was written for Enduring Minds, The Foundation. The nonprofit organization was started by the Author Essence Unique. Through Enduring Minds, Essence strives to provide resources & help people who endure illnesses as the one talked about in this book. If that's you or someone you know or you'd like to learn more about Enduring Minds, The Foundation check us out at www.enduringminds.com

Hey Allen, I just woke in so much pain!

Aww Emilia, why are you so tired?
I hope it's not what I think it is.

I haven't been feeling well lately, Emilia says.

If it is, we'll handle it honey, why don't you lay down and I'll take care of Ezra today, Allen says.

Good morning Daddy,
where's Mommy Ezra wonders.

Good morning Ezra, Daddy missed you,
did you sleep well ? Mommy is in bed,
and isn't feeling well today.

But Mommy was sick yesterday.
I wanted to have a tea party today,
she loves tea parties.

I know baby, says Allen.
Mommies get sick
and need a break,
she'll be able to play soon.

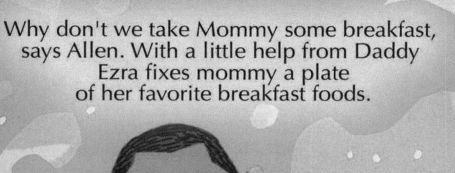

Why don't we take Mommy some breakfast, says Allen. With a little help from Daddy Ezra fixes mommy a plate of her favorite breakfast foods.

Proudly carrying Mommy's breakfast,
Ezra pauses and starts to wonder.
Why is Mommy in bed
all the time now? Ezra asks.

Because Ezra, like I said,
mom's get sick and needs lots of rest
to raise strong young boys.

That makes sense. I just want to play
with Mommy again.

I know son , let's take Mommy her breakfast
and make her smile, your smile always
makes her feel better!

Honey, I think we need to go ahead
and call your doctor, says Allen.

Ezra's parents call the doctor and learn
mom needs to have surgery again.

Honey, I'm scared, Emilia says.
I can't believe after ten years,
I have to have brain surgery again.

How do I explain this to Ezra?
What about our business?

Allen tells Emilia, We got this, we've been through this before, and we'll get through this now. We just have to talk to Ezra about it. Kids are stronger and smarter than we give them credit for. He'll understand.
And our business will be fine;
we're a team. We got this.

Mommy you look like you've been crying,
Am I having a baby brother? Ezra asks.

Mommy and Daddy have something to tell you.
Do you remember when Mommy told you
how before you were born, Mommy was sick?
Mommy's sickness comes back sometimes,
just like how you lose your ball,
and then you find it again. Unfortunately
Mommy's sickness has come back now.

Okay Mommy, you have to take some medicine
like the nasty stuff you give me when I'm sick?

Mommy smiles. Well, my sickness is called a chronic illness. I will always have it, and we have to manage it as a family.

Sometimes, Mommy has to have something called brain surgery. My condition is called Pseudotumor Cerebri, that means my brain has too much fluid, and it messes with stuff. When that fluid messes with too much stuff, I get tired, it can be scary but it's always okay. My doctor cuts some of my hair then makes a small cut in my head, then puts a tube in Mommy's head to take the fluid away.

Your brain has too much what, mommy??

Too much fluid like water. You know how
you get a cup of water with dinner?
Well, that cup can only hold so much water.
That's like Mommy's brain. It can only hold
much before it makes a mess or makes Mommy
sick. I know it isn't very easy to understand.
But, know that Mommy's brain gets big,
and Mommy's doctor makes it normal again,
even if only for a little while.

Mommy may be in the hospital, and we'll
have to take care of her when she gets home.
Says Daddy.

I can't wait to be your doctor, Mommy. I hope
you get better soon. I think I understand,
Mommy's brain gets big because
it has too much water. It hurts but gets better.

Mommy, can I get a pseudotumor too? Ezra asks.

I don't know. Kids can get illnesses that
are chronic too. I pray that you never do,
but anyone can get it. I want you to remember
that there are a lot of people, like Mommy,
who are sick. And you can't tell with your eyes,
so you must be kind to people,
help when you can, and respect everyone
whether they have an illness or not.

Dr.Fleeming meets Ezra and Daddy at the hospital
Your mom's surgery went well,
once she heals up, she should be all better.

Ezra gets excited. I can't wait to play with mommy

Now, Ezra, I want you to understand
this may happen again. Mommy may not be
feeling well sometimes, but I did my best to make
sure she gets better now. She's not ready to play
yet, but she will be soon.

That's cool, I know why my Mommy likes you;
you're a nice doctor. I want to be a doctor
when I grow tall like you. Ezra says.

Thank you, Dr. Fleeming.
says Daddy.

Can I take Mommy her medicine?

Yes, said Daddy, but quietly. Peek in the room and see if Mommy is sleeping first. Shhh...

Emelia gives Ezra a big warm hug.
I feel pretty good for only being home a week!

That's great, Mommy. I'm so glad your brain has so much fluid that I get to take care of you.
Now that your brain is fixed,
can I have a little brother, please?

Printed in the USA
CPSIA information can be obtained
at www.ICGtesting.com
LVHW072008081123
763421LV00015BA/123